The

LIGHTHOUSE FAMILY

THE OCTOPUS

The

LIGHTHOUSE FAMILY

THE OCTOPUS

BY CYNTHIA RYLANT

ILLUSTRATED BY PRESTON McDANIELS

BEACH LANE BOOKS

New York   London   Toronto   Sydney   New Delhi

BEACH LANE BOOKS

An imprint of Simon & Schuster Children's Publishing Division

1230 Avenue of the Americas, New York, New York 10020

This book is a work of fiction. Any references to historical events, real people, or real places are used fictitiously. Other names, characters, places, and events are products of the author's imagination, and any resemblance to actual events or places or persons, living or dead, is entirely coincidental.

Text copyright © 2005 by Cynthia Rylant

Illustrations copyright © 2005 by Preston McDaniels

BEACH LANE BOOKS is a trademark of Simon & Schuster, Inc.

For information about special discounts for bulk purchases, please contact Simon & Schuster Special Sales at 1-866-506-1949 or business@simonandschuster.com.

The Simon & Schuster Speakers Bureau can bring authors to your live event. For more information or to book an event, contact the Simon & Schuster Speakers Bureau at 1-866-248-3049 or visit our website at www.simonspeakers.com.

Also available in a Beach Lane Books hardcover edition

The text for this book was set in Centaur.

The illustrations for this book were rendered in graphite.

Manufactured in the United States of America

0216 OFF

First Beach Lane Books paperback edition March 2016

2 4 6 8 10 9 7 5 3 1

The Library of Congress has cataloged the hardcover edition as follows:

Rylant, Cynthia.

The lighthouse family : the octopus / Cynthia Rylant ; illustrated by Preston McDaniels.— 1st ed.   p. cm.

Summary: Whistler and Lila, two of the mice children who live in a lighthouse, meet a young octopus when they visit the beach during low tide.

ISBN 978-0-689-86246-5 (hc) — ISBN 978-0-689-86314-1 (pbk)

ISBN 978-1-4424-9938-6 (eBook)

[1. Mice—Fiction. 2. Octopuses—Fiction. 3. Seashore—Fiction. 4. Animals—Fiction. 5. Lighthouses—Fiction.] I. McDaniels, Preston, ill. II. Title.

PZ7.R982Lc 2005   [Fic]—dc22   2004028506

For Kim Sam Ton That
—*P. McD.*

CONTENTS

1. The Garden

Perched on an island cliff, high above the deep waters of the ocean, a lighthouse stands steady and strong. Its great lamp shines across the waves day and night, guiding sailors on their journeys home.

This lighthouse is well loved, and not only by the sailors who watch carefully for its beacon in the night. It is also well loved by the family who lives there.

This is a happy family. Pandora, the cat, and Seabold, the dog, are raising three mouse-children, in addition to keeping the light. The children are Whistler, Lila, and baby Tiny.

The members of this family somehow found each other in this large, wide world. Pandora had

lived four lonely years as a lighthouse keeper when she discovered Seabold washed upon her shore, battered by the storm that had tossed him there.

Pandora tended Seabold back to health. But just as Seabold was planning his return to the sailor's life, he and Pandora found the children, lost and adrift at sea. The little mice had fled from an orphanage and, like Seabold, had been blown by a storm to the sanctuary of Pandora's lighthouse.

Within the keeper's cottage they each found kindness and comfort and the sudden pleasure of warm food and company. And there with Pandora they decided to stay. Even Seabold, the wanderer.

A long island winter was behind them now. It was spring again, and so much to do. Spring is a lively time around a lighthouse.

Whistler was shaping a bean trellis into the form of a cat, which delighted Pandora.

"By July the vines will have grown," said Whistler, "and the cat will show nicely."

"Brilliant," said Seabold. Seabold was busy

planting carrots and beets. Seabold didn't much like beets, but he planted them for Lila, who liked to dip the doll clothes she sewed into beet juice to dye them a lovely red. She also used carrot tops to make a nice yellow.

Baby Tiny was big enough now to play in the lighthouse yard. But Seabold was so worried a strong gust of wind might blow her off the cliff that he tied her to Pandora's clothesline with a long length of woolen yarn. Tiny happily stacked her wooden blocks and scallop shells and the tiny puffins that Seabold had made.

In the fields behind the lighthouse the wild irises were budding, as were the poppies and prim-rose, and bluebells. And on the dunes the beach morning glories had begun to creep. In June when the morning glory vines were thick, Whistler and Lila planned to play hide-and-seek among the white blossoms.

For now they were happy to concentrate on Pandora's garden. While Whistler constructed his trellis, Lila made beetle houses with small piles of rocks, and she collected fresh water from the rain barrel into shells, placing these near the houses so the beetles might have a drink. Birds, too.

"Tonight is the full moon, children," said Pandora as she walked through the garden with an apron of mint.

"Oh good," said Lila, settling a shell into the ground. "Everything will glow."

"Yes," said Seabold. "This moon will also bring the lowest tide of the year."

"It will?" asked Whistler.

"Indeed," answered Seabold. "There should be new things to see in the estuary when the water pulls back."

"We should explore!" said Lila.

"Definitely!" said Whistler. The children loved walking over the estuary at low tide, making tiny footprints in the mud as they looked at starfish and anemones left behind by the receding water.

"Tomorrow morning you may pack a bit of breakfast and go out early while Pandora and I trim the wicks," said Seabold. He said this cheerfully,

for Seabold quite liked his keeper duties.

"Tiny will keep us company, won't you, Tiny?" Seabold added. The baby smiled at him. Seabold quite liked Tiny, too. He often carried her about as he did his chores, tucking her in the roll of his wool cap or fitting her into his vest pocket.

"But you must be very cautious, children," said Pandora, pouring the mint from her apron onto a netted screen to dry.

"You must remember not to turn your back to the sea as you explore the estuary," she said. "Always watch for the tide coming in, and be sure to return to the shore well ahead of it."

"We'll be careful," said Whistler.

"We promise," added Lila.

"And will you bring back some sugar kelp?" asked Pandora with a smile. "For lunch?"

"Of course!" said the children.

The lighthouse family *loved* sugar kelp. Lunch would be wonderful.

2. *To the Shore*

Early the next morning Pandora packed Whistler and Lila's twine bags with gooseberry biscuits, small red apples, and wooden flasks filled with tea. The children pulled on their slickers and they each kissed Tiny good-bye. (Tiny had been watching them from inside a sifter on the kitchen table.)

"Don't forget," reminded Pandora.

"Never turn our backs to the sea," said Whistler.

"Right," said Seabold, coming down the steps from the lantern room with several cleaning cloths in his hand.

"And remember to be quiet and friendly," he added. "The tide isn't often this low, so some of the creatures you meet may feel uncertain because they are usually covered by water."

"We will be as quiet as quiet can be," said Lila.

"I'm sure you will, dears," said Pandora, opening the door for them. "Just be home for lunch."

"Yes, Pandora," said Lila.

"See you soon!" said Whistler.

And carrying their breakfast bags, the children headed down to the shore.

3. The Octopus

When the children reached the shore, they were delighted to see how far away the water lay and how much more beach there was to explore.

"It feels as if we have a whole new island," said Lila as they walked out upon the hard, wet sand.

Whistler stepped gingerly around a small starfish.

"Quiet and friendly," he reminded Lila. "Quiet and friendly."

Lila pointed far out to the edge of the estuary, where the ocean gently lapped as it pulled itself away.

"We've never been all the way out there," she said.

"Let's go," said Whistler.

The children ventured farther and farther out

over the estuary. As they walked, sea squirts shot water up all around them and crabs scuttled and starfish watched.

"The mud is getting softer," said Lila, lifting her foot.

"It hasn't dried in the sun yet," said Whistler.

Whistler and Lila stopped to look into the little pools of water the tide had left behind.

"Goodness," said Lila, gazing at a giant green anemone. "I've never met one of these."

"And I've never met one of these," said Whistler, pointing to an orange sea cucumber.

Someone tapped Whistler on the leg.

"Have you ever met one of me?" a voice asked.

"Ah!" Whistler jumped in surprise. "Who said that?"

He and Lila peered behind them into a small, dark pool of water. "I think I see a pair of eyes," said Lila. "Or maybe doorknobs."

"Where?" asked Whistler, bending closer to the water.

A small tentacle reached up from the pool and tapped him on the nose.

"*Ah!*" Whistler jumped again.

"Hey!" said Lila. "It's an octopus!"

They watched as two large yellow eyes, which did indeed look like doorknobs, rose to the water's surface. The yellow eyes belonged to a small, baggy body that sported eight long tentacles.

One of the tentacles waved hello.

"My name is Cleo," said the octopus. "I'm sorry I made you jump."

"Oh, that's quite all right," said Whistler. "That was a good trick. I'm Whistler and this is my sister Lila."

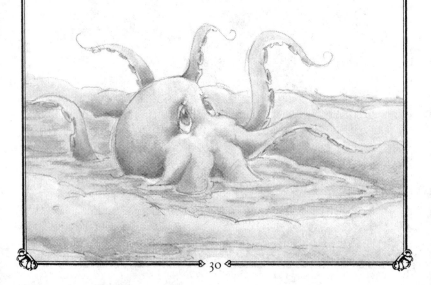

"Pleased to meet you," said Lila, stepping nearer the octopus. As she drew closer, something amazing happened.

"You changed!" said Lila. "Now you have stripes!"

"Oops," said Cleo. "They're *your* stripes," he said, pointing to Lila's slicker. "Sometimes I blend without thinking."

"Amazing!" said Whistler.

"Well, I'm still practicing on stripes," said Cleo. "But I do reds and greens quite well."

"May we see?" asked Lila.

"Do you have something red with you?" asked Cleo.

Lila and Whistler looked at each other.

"Apples!" said Whistler.

He pulled his apple from the twine bag and held it out to Cleo.

The octopus turned a wonderful red.

"Oh my goodness!" said Lila.

Cleo assumed his original brown shade.

"I like colors," he said, "but I'm too shy to be flashy."

"I never thought we'd meet an octopus in the estuary," said Whistler.

"Yes," said Lila. "Usually there are only creatures who squirt or stare."

"I made a mistake," said Cleo. "That's why I'm here in this little pool."

"A mistake?" asked Lila.

"The tide pulled away so quickly," said the octopus. "I was resting in this hole and when I popped my head up, the ocean had left me behind!"

"Oh dear," said Lila.

"Don't worry," Whistler told the octopus. "The tide will come back and carry you out to sea again."

"Shall we keep you company until it does?" asked Lila.

"Would you?" asked Cleo. "It's a bit boring just sitting here. I don't know how the starfish do it."

"They solve problems," said Whistler.

"Pardon me?" asked Cleo.

"I once asked a starfish what he does all day," explained Whistler, "and he said, 'I solve problems.'"

"Oh," said Cleo. "What sort of problems?"

"Well," said Whistler, "he said to me, 'Today it's a mouse problem.'"

"Oh." The octopus thought a moment. "I'm not sure," Cleo said, "but I think perhaps he was being rude."

"I think so too," said Lila.

Whistler agreed. Then he pulled open his twine bag.

"Have you ever had a gooseberry biscuit?" he asked Cleo.

Whistler broke a biscuit into four pieces and placed each piece on one of Cleo's tentacles.

Pop, pop, pop, pop. The little octopus popped each piece into his mouth.

"Mmmmm." He smiled. "Thank you."

Lila looked out toward the water.

"Whistler," she said, "I think the tide has started coming in."

Whistler looked at the line of water now slowly lapping its way to shore.

"Oops," he said. "We'd better go. Cleo, will you swim over to the lighthouse to visit us sometime?"

"I'd love to!" said Cleo.

"We'd better hurry," said Lila. "The tide seems to be edging in fast."

She picked up her bag and tried to take a step.

"I'm stuck!" she said. "I can't move my feet!"

Whistler knelt down and tried to lift Lila's foot out of the mud.

"Your foot won't budge!" he said. "Pull—pull hard!"

Lila tried with all her strength to move her feet.

"I'm stuck!" she said. "And the tide is coming in!"

"I'm strong," said Cleo. "Maybe I can lift you out."

He wrapped a tentacle around Lila's waist and pulled.

"It isn't working!" said Lila. "The mud has hardened all around me and it won't let me go."

"We have to soften it up," said Whistler. "We have to get it all wet again."

"Hurry!" said Lila "Think of something!"

"I *have!*" said Cleo. And he turned his body until a funnel-shaped part of it was pointing at Lila.

"Hold on!" said Cleo. He sucked water into the funnel, then shot it out in a strong spray all over Lila.

"Great!" said Whistler. "Keep going!"

Cleo sprayed and sprayed until Lila, and all the mud surrounding her, was soaking wet.

Lila lifted one foot out of the mud. *Thook.* Then another.

She gave a deep, drippy sigh of relief.

"Thank you, Cleo," she said. "Thank you."

Whistler grabbed Lila's hand to run back to shore and home.

"Come visit us, Cleo!" Whistler called as they

ran. "Tomorrow afternoon!"

And the two mouse-children ran quickly to safety, away from the water, which the little octopus couldn't wait to swim in again.

4. Home

Whistler and Lila arrived home with four muddy feet, no sugar kelp, and some sneezes (Lila's). Pandora met them at the door and knew right away that their morning had been an eventful one. (Another adventure, Seabold would have said, had he not been up in the lantern room with Tiny.)

Pandora brought the children in and sat them down by the stove, and then she put their feet in pans of nice warm water and draped warm woolen cloths over their heads.

"But *my* head isn't wet," said Whistler. "Only Lila got sprayed."

"Every head wants to be warmed," said Pandora, bringing a pot of tea to the table. "And how did you come to be sprayed, Lila dear?"

"It was an octopus," said Lila.

Pandora set down the teapot. She looked calmly at the children.

"I think Seabold might like to hear this story," she said. And she called him down from the lantern room.

When Seabold came down, with Tiny on his shoulder, everyone gathered for tea while the children explained how they came to meet an octopus and how the octopus had saved Lila.

"Astounding," said Seabold. "And very good thinking for a baby."

"A baby?" asked Whistler.

"Yes, of course," said Seabold. "Any octopus found in a tidal pool so small would be a child."

"You mean Cleo will grow bigger?" asked Lila.

"Oh, *much* bigger," said Seabold.

"We should thank the child in some way," said Pandora.

"Yes," said Lila. "He's a hero for saving me."

"I invited him to visit us tomorrow afternoon," said Whistler.

"Perfect," said Pandora. "I'll make a nice big lunch—"

"He likes gooseberry biscuits," interrupted Whistler.

"—which will include gooseberry biscuits," finished Pandora with a smile.

After tea Pandora sent the children to nap away their exciting morning, first settling them into their sock-bed, then tying a flannel scarf about Lila's head.

"I'm sorry I got stuck and forgot to bring home the sugar kelp," Lila whispered softly.

Pandora purred and patted her lovingly.

"You brought home *you*," said Pandora. "That is all this family ever asks, dear."

Lila smiled and went instantly to sleep.

5. A Family

The next afternoon it was quite thrilling when Seabold spotted not one, but three octopi from the window of the lantern room.

"The octopi have arrived!" he called down the stairs to the children who were helping Pandora in the kitchen.

"*Octopi?*" repeated Whistler.

As Pandora finished preparing a picnic lunch, Whistler and Lila ran down to the shore. There they found Cleo swimming in the waves, and they knew right away he was indeed a child, for the tentacled creatures with him were *much* larger than he.

"I brought my parents!" Cleo called.

The three octopi came as close to shore as they

could and Whistler and Lila were delighted to be introduced to Cleo's parents, Hancock and Florence. Florence stayed hidden in the water mostly. Only her eyes broke the surface.

"My mother is shy," said Cleo. "We're *all* shy. But I really wanted my parents to meet you."

Lila put on her best, most inviting smile and welcomed them.

"We are so very happy to have you here," she told Hancock and Florence. "Your son is a *hero*."

Upon hearing those words, all three octopi turned red.

"Oops," said Lila.

"We're just proud, little mouse," said Hancock. "We're just proud of our boy."

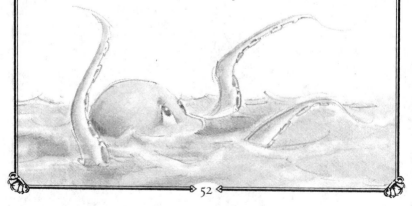

"They turned red because I did," said Cleo. "You know how we blend."

"We hope you'll meet us in the sea cave over there for lunch," said Whistler. "Will you?"

Florence popped her head up.

"We'd be pleased to," she said.

Then she popped it back down.

"Wonderful!" said Lila.

And before long, the lighthouse family and the octopus family were all gathered in the sea cave, enjoying lunch and each other.

Pandora had prepared a wonderful meal of fluffy gooseberry biscuits, a salad of chickweed, mushrooms, and apples, and for dessert rhubarb potpies.

"I shall never enjoy kelp again," said Hancock as he filled his mouth with another piece of pie.

Cleo's mother, Florence, had brought a pearl bracelet for Pandora, a gift for their hostess.

"The pearls came from our shipwreck," explained Cleo.

"Your shipwreck?" asked Whistler.

"We live in a shipwreck," said Cleo. "Didn't I mention that?"

"Fantastic!" said Whistler.

And so the new friends lingered in the sea cave all afternoon. Seabold and Hancock traded stories about the grumpiest fish they'd met (Seabold: a blowfish; Hancock: a squid). Florence told Pandora about the healing properties of sea carrots, while Tiny ran up and down all of Cleo's tentacles. And Whistler and Lila gathered pale violet daisies from the cave's entrance, bringing everyone a small, fragrant bouquet.

Everything was good this day. It was always good to make new friends.